Julio Cortázar

Diary of Andrés Fava

Translated from the Spanish by Anne McLean

a r c h i p e l a g o   b o o k s

Library of Congress Control Number: 2005923938

Archipelago Books
25 Jay Street #203
Brooklyn, NY 11201
www.archipelagobooks.org

Distributed by Consortium Book Sales and Distribution
1045 Westgate Drive
St. Paul, MN 55114
www.cbsd.com

Diary of Andrés Fava

Jacket art: *Improvisation 30*, Wassily Kandinsky, 1913
Copyright © 2004 Artists Rights Society (ARS), New York, NY / ADAGP, Paris

This publication is made possible with a regrant from the Council of Literary
Magazines and Presses, supported by public funds from the New York State
Council on the Arts, a state agency.

NYSCA

Diary of Andrés Fava

This mental mucus is driving me mad. The Japanese blow their noses on paper too. "Diary of life," day by day; day-to-day life. Poor soul, you'll end up speaking journalese. You already do now and then.

An encouraging little tango:

> "Go on, don't stop,
> Just keep playing along—,"

And this line by Eduardo Lozano:

> *My heart, imitation moss.*

What they tend to call "classic" is always a product achieved by the sacrifice of truth to beauty.

Waiting for a bus at Chacarita. Storm brewing, low sky over the cemetery. Keeping my place in line I spend a long time staring at the tops of the trees that lead up to the peristyle. A continuous line of crowns (deepened and purified by the gray sky), waving gracefully as if at the edge of the clouds. High up on the peristyle, the enormous angel hovers among the silhouettes of trees; it looks as though he's resting his foot on the leaves. A second of perfect beauty, then shouts, shoves, climb onto the bus, move further back, fifteen or ten centavo ticket, life. Farewell, my beauties, one day I'll rest snugly wrapped in that delicate lace, which will protect me evermore from buses.

(The gentle idiocy of some sentences. Verbal sighs.)

I'm only interested in the primitives and my contemporaries, Simone Martini and Gischia, Guillaume de Machault and Alban Berg. From the sixteenth century to the nineteenth I have the impression that art was neither alive enough nor dead enough.

Rimbaud, "ambulatory" poet. Fatigue: stimulus for revelation to jump up and settle in. Idleness begets idleness, and so on. Yesterday I was going home on the 168, squeezing in among people and odors. Suddenly the visitation, the piercing happiness. *To have the wordless poem*, entirely formulated and waiting; to know it. Without a theme, without words, *and knowing it*. A single pure line:

Saintly, like a swallow.

But so rarely—Since the evening I heard that line (and another two the following morning), a deaf opacity, feeling myself full of vivid matter, engaged with itself, satisfied pondering. I vegetate, I come and go, take refuge in reading. Eliot, Chandler, Colette, Priestly, Connolly . . .

I listen to Laurence Olivier's recording of *Henry V* again. It's always time to die, but these discs with their timeless spiral hold an instant of eternity. It's not in the words, it's not exactly Will or Larry, or the felicity Walton adds with his music. The eternal takes form through man's action. It was all necessary, and that a vocation should launch Olivier, and behind him England, cinema, the moment, the war, the atmosphere

that did affright the air at Agincourt —

And suddenly, as in the conception, or in the meeting of two words that ignite in poetry, the eternal: an attitude, a gesture, *and he babbled o'er green fields,* and the Constable, and that boy murmuring: some crying, *some swearing, some calling for a surgeon* — Everything met; the seven colors provide the whiteness that obliterates them in perfection, in *uncolored color, Eternity.*

When you're not an intellectual, the inconsistency and poverty of ideas makes you fear that everything written (except one poem, perhaps one story) is useless and ridiculous. Ideas, that is the establishment of relationships, bridgeheads, bridges. Surrounded by books, I lean over a flower left on my desk. Its blind translucent pupil looks at me; I think if it were really looking at me, it wouldn't see me.

Maybe this diary is an Argentine preoccupation; like the café—oral diary of life—strings of women, easy deals and tame sadness. How difficult a coherent construction seems here, any order or a style. Besides, to write a diary you *must be worthy of one*. Like Gide or T. E. Lawrence. A diary, the lacy froth that flowers on the surface of boiling syrup. *To seethe*, yes, but not in empty pans. If I'd lived well, if I'd died well, if this place where I exist were solid and not the self-pitying jelly I love to eat, then yes; then to put the things left unsaid into words, the little froth, surplus to the struggle.

Along the Santa Fe *Trail*—Bing Crosby sings and I'm struck once more by that surprise of any Spanish word stuck in the middle of an English or French construction. Suddenly, in just that instant, the discovery of the word in all its virginity; but then it's blotted out, then it's back to the thing I know (or rather that I don't know, that I just use).

I meet a friend who's bad-tempered and nervous because of a problem at work that's harrying him. From outside, from the edge of his desk, it's easy to measure the absurdity of this preoccupation about something that doesn't even touch him (vicariously living someone else's problem: misfortune of a good worker, of an honest manager). I wonder whether it occurs to him to suddenly consider the absurd, as a comparison with the cosmic, whether he sometimes takes a step back so the monster in front of his eyes turns back into the fly hovering in the air. Techniques, nothing more. Baruch Spinoza, what a swine. When someone died, an unmoved acquaintance said to me:

—I don't let things like this get the better of me; I take immediate refuge in metaphysics.

—The deceased was obviously not your lover—I answered.

If only . . . I've always admired Laforgue's exact, annihilating sense of *universal proportion*. The only French poet to look at reality on a planetary scale. Keeping an awareness of totality when faced with a missed train, a stain on a suit, reducing the incident to less than nothing. But it's clear the deceased was not your lover. Oh, Andrés, your head or your liver is starting to ache, and that insignificance blocks out *il sole e l'altre stele*. You lose a life like the ones already killed off, and to hell with the universe. The ego refuses to compromise, an eye devouring the world—without seeing it.

Clara and Juan remember Abelito sometimes, but I forget more easily now that I so rarely run into him. Instead another comes to mind,

and that's just how to say it because that's how it happens: the guy opens the door and there he is,

an Abel I saw a couple of times in Mendoza who gave me a fright. I think I write in order to have a hedonistic experience of exquisite fear; then it was marred by a feeling of danger and repulsion. I rang the bell (I was looking for a room, saw an ad, it was a house of several stories towards the north end of Avenida San Martín, in that part that pretties itself up with poplars and Syrian shops) and the door was opened by a being who hadn't been born to open doors. He had blue pyjamas and the palest face I'd ever seen, a terrifying *pierrot* standing firmly out against the darkness of the vestibule. Dilated pupils, light eyes (but I don't remember the color, or never saw) looking at me with a bland intensity, lapping up my face in a silence that I guiltily lengthened. Then I mentioned the ad, and the being stepped aside to let me in and said: "Go on up." The voice was the eyes, as if algae could speak: as inhuman as a parrot, but at the same time containing the being; voice of the witness who says the revealing word. I went up, certain I wouldn't stay in the house. Upstairs was an old woman in the very corridor for her French accent and hands full of rings. I was taken to my possible room, she talked and the being followed us, watching me; now I remember his amusing body, the blue arc his pyjamas outlined in the doorframe: dancer in repose.

The woman cut in to send him away curtly: "Off you go, Abel." The being disappeared slipping away sideways, watching me until he was gone. My feelings must have shown because the woman lowered her voice to tell me: "Abel will clean up your room, and you just give him a tip each month. You don't have to pay him any mind because he's a bit sickly—" (I don't think she said "sickly" but I forget the word, there's a censoring that erases it from the center of this clear memory.)

I agreed to let her have my answer that same evening and said goodbye. As I was going down the stairs, Abel appeared at my side. He slipped along a step ahead or one behind, *watching me.* It was horrible how he laid me bare. At the door I said, "Good afternoon," but he didn't answer. (Years later, seeing Barrault mime Pierrot, I felt again the atrocious weight of that silence. But Abel was threat, a swamp in the air, waiting.)

Time went by, I was living in another rooming house. One night I was returning very late, delaying the moment of sleep; it was hot, the moon was up, the streets fragrant. Halfway down an almost entirely dark block, I heard laughing, singing and shouting all at once, a throng of words and hysterical shrieks, quick outbursts were cut off only to start straight up again. I saw Abel come leaping and pirouetting, the bright white of Palm Beach beneath the moon, his face a white mask with shadowy craters. He was unleashed, erupted, the absolutely inverted Abel running his amok through the city. A group of people must've laughed at him when he passed; so he broke away, came along proclaiming himself, crazed and free, perhaps on drugs; he didn't even see me as he passed, he hopped and hummed happily, laughing as he leapt, finally began a song and turned the corner.

I never saw him again, maybe that's why I remember so well.

The incalculable function of certain books in a life still porous, attentive, expectant. I'm thinking of the *Anthologie des poètes de la NRF* I bought in 1939 (perhaps before), which instantly became pivotal, a delegation of the unknown clamoring and gnawing night and day. The dazzle of unsuspected poems, prestige of names still unattached to any biography or portrait (Jouve, Saint-John Perse; and later, in 1945, to see a photo of Perse, that face of a jovial shop-keeper, like the face of Rouault that I only just met in a film . . .). And Kra's anthology too, read in 1935, badly understood because my French was so deplorable then. Double magic, madness: Rimbaud, Anne, Anne, *fuis sur ton âne;* I can see myself copying out *La comédie de la soif* before returning the book; and all of Mallarmé, absolute mystery with sudden delight: *un sens trop précis rature ta vague littérature*—And the others, soon isolated from so many poems without resonance: Valéry, Apollinaire, Carco (and this one, afterwards, entirely discovered with *Jésus-la-Caille* and *La bohème et mon coeur*). Nights of plazas, cappuccinos, ardent nothings; crying with Léon-Paul Fargue: *Et peut-être qu'un jour, pour de nou-*

veaux amis . . . Love looking up from a cup of coffee; the price of a silence, the walk home past tree-lined avenues and cats. Reverdy, whom no one in my group liked, and Michaux, and the exquisite Supervielle—I just think of the book, the big letters *NRF,* and up jumps Perse, up jumps Jouve. And when I say Kra (with the orange of the cover) then Rimbaud, fulminating and rabid, Cendrars and Laforgue—later in those two yellow volumes from Mercure, then Laforgue, such a sweet clown, tickling, moaning, a cat rubbing up against your legs, gentle scratching, curling up into a ball and then they bring you the newspaper and she has died, but in any case tomorrow the temperature will continue rising gradually.

Definition of mystery: The cage was empty with the door open, and when they came to look there was a rose at the back, with its stem in a little glass of water, and you could tell it had just been cut.

Certain caresses, gentle grazes—Colette speaking them, and also Rosamond Lehman when they're more furtive and distant. And gestures . . . *For such gestures, one falls hopelessly in love for a lifetime . . .* Wasn't that how it was, Rose Macaulay?

Certain caresses, the barely material very tip of a finger brushing the nape of a neck, where the sweetest kind of tingle resides.

Return to the fold.—Greek antiquity or the obsession with return. The great tragedies detonate *upon return:* Odysseus, Agamemnon, Oedipus.

> *Quand ce jeune homme revint chez lui*
> *Et digue don don, et digue dondaine*—

Whereas the biblical tragedy is leaving: Moses, Joseph—and Jesus, the one who leaves, the one who doesn't lock the door on the way out.

Joy is saved for the return, for the prodigal son, Abraham and Isaac, David—

To write: sublimate, surrogate, substitute . . . It's almost a cliché now, we know it all too well, in other words, we forget it. Might it not be time to better analyze this brilliant truth of psychology? Truth is always a valid system of relations. It seems relations between a writer and his hormones, his complexes and his fetters, are well comprehended by this truth that gives us the lovely formula: Literature = Substitutive Route. But this truth might be passé now, not because it wasn't one, but because the writer's relations with himself and his circumstances could be changing.

They say—and one smiles—"Language keeps me from expressing what I think, what I feel." It would be truer to say: "What I think, what I feel, keeps me from getting to language." Between my thinking and me, language raises objections? No. It's my thinking that comes between my language and me.

Therefore there is no other way out except to hoist language up until it reaches total autonomy. In great poets, the words don't carry the thought along with them; they are the thought. Which, of course, is no longer thought but Word.

Read *The* already untimely *Time Machine*. Oh little Weena, *animalito humano*, only living thing in an unbearable tale. Writing tiny music, games and rounds for Weena. Feeling her in one's arms when hesitantly crossing a darkened chamber alone.

Like the poor drum, who encourages beatings with its elastic rebound.

Stroking her hair is one thing, finding one in your soup is quite another. (Heard from the Chronicler.)

Unilateralism, man's one-way track. You feel that living means projecting yourself in one direction (and time is the objectification of this unique line). You can do nothing but advance down a corridor where the windows or the pauses are incidental to what really matters: the march towards an end that (since we ourselves are the corridor) gets further and further away from our starting point, the intermediate stages—It's an obscure point and I don't know how to make it: feeling that my life and I are two things, and that if it were possible to take off life like a jacket, hang it up for a while on the back of a chair, then we could jump from one place to the next, escape from the uniform and continuous projection. Then put it back on, or find another. It's so *boring* that we have only one life, or that life should have only one way of happening. No matter how we fill it with events, pretty it up with a well-planned and executed destiny, *there's only one pattern:* fifteen years old, twenty-five, forty—the corridor. We conduct life as we conduct our eyes, wearing it whichever way suits us; eyes see the future of space, since life's always a step ahead of time.

Hylozoism, man's anxiousness to live as a crab, as a stone, to see-from-atop-a-palm-tree. That's why the poet *displaces.*

What pains me is knowing I'm going down the same corridor, a single model since time began. There are no individuals except by accident; for what really matters, we deserve the telephone directory, levelled like that, symmetrical columbariums like that,

the same thing, the same corridor.

This isn't misanthropy. Nor haggling with life, lovely thing. It's my share of universal being. Pantheism? Pananthropism. But not because I want to be everything, live-the-world; what I want is for the world to be me, for there to be no limits to my living trace. Argos, all eyes?

All the eyes, Argos.

Another definition of the terrible *señor:* "Man is the animal that takes stock."

Property is life-sized stock-taking. I have ten hectares, a dapple-gray horse, a little heart-shaped cloud.

There comes a day when memory is more robust. I do indeed have a dapple-gray horse, but I also had Refucilo, I had Mangangá, I had a colt with dawn coursing through his veins, I had Prenda, sugar at a gallop . . .

Even the clouds: here they are, mine. The clouds over Llanquihue, one January evening in 1942; the big slate cloud that overwhelmed me in Tilcara, filling the river with yellow muck; the sexual nimbus clouds, snow at their backs and cold delirium over the indigo-tinted water that is the midday sky in Mendoza la *pulida;* the clouds in a song Juan played around with years ago; and the ones I put into four lines as a treat for Pampa, my dead dog:

> *You must be lying by an empty bed*
> *Sure your owner will catch up one night*
> *In the meantime you'll eat the smallest clouds,*
> *Greedy for sugar I can no longer bestow.*

Yes, Jean-Paul: man is the sum of his actions. But yours is a dynamic approach to this melancholy integration: man is the sum of his stock-taking. (And thus *The Great Lover* by Brooke, and thus Proust, Rosamond Lehmann, Colette, bees sipping time—is it not certainly so?)

Lazy sketch of stock-taking: I had *Pélleas,* I had a tiny mandolin that fit in the palm of my hand and was given to me by someone who met an innocent death; I had a cat at the age when little separates us from the secret silence of animals, from their unambitious wisdom. I had collections of stamps, of clippings, of stories; I had a night in the high Paraná, lying on my back on the deck of a dirty little boat, devoured by stars; I had *A Farewell to Arms,* Helen Hayes; and one night when I was suffering, in front of a big open window, I had the caress of a hand that came from the shadows, without my ever knowing who, of those with me, merged so purely with my pain. I had—(How much better this certainty than all the bastards: "I never had . . .")

Read *Demian*. Strange how there are certain aversions prior to a reading, almost always corroborated when you cede to the suggestions of third parties. Will Bernanos, Pritchett, Orwell, Plisnier seem as disagreeable to me as this Hermann Hesse? *Demian* could have been exactly all that it isn't. Notes immediately following the reading: 1. Author's probable narrative talent—don't forget I read it in Spanish—at the service of a stupid tale, *implausible* (with that ultimate implausibility, which has nothing to do with lack of logic, exaggeration or fantasy). Sinclair is any one of us crossing the puddle of adolescence: with the usual splashes. But Demian—his famous "guide"—turns out to be the stupidest creature of the superman genre ever produced by the German novel (even if Hesse is a Swiss citizen). As for Eva, inexpressible monster, fetish object coming in and out without ever knowing *what's cooking* . . . Mother and son explain far too much of Hesse's mental confusion. Elements of this cocktail: the *om*, Abraxas (another one!), magic, various demonstrations of telepathy, volition, etc., mixed with the sentimentality of a seamstress (tears, swoons, symbolic drunkenness, not to mention the supreme mediocrity after

Demian: Pistorius). 2. The theme *(to thine own self be true)* would fit in fewer pages, aside from the fact that it's older than Demian—I suppose a kind of shameful Ashaverus. The parallel matter of Sinclair's sentimental and moral education, isn't badly told. But, good grief, after Rimbaud, Radiguet, even Alain Fournier . . . 3. The superman-à-la-USA bit is deplorable. The part where Sinclair goes down to Demian's garden and finds him training to fight a Japanese man is so ridiculous it could have come out of an Alan Ladd film. (In the following chapter Hesse doesn't neglect to inform us that the Japanese man took a beating.)

And now, really: what is *Demian?* A perceptibly homosexual novel, so why these esoteric disguises, this no-Beatrice, no-Eve, no one (none). We know perfectly well what Sinclair wanted and needed, what he gets on the last page: for Demian to kiss him on the lips. My God, how I would respect this book if I'd seen in its author a fraction of the courage that brings *Death in Venice* off perfectly. But no, he had to trot out the old allegorical to-do, Abraxas and those silly women. Turn poor Demian into a puppet, a dummy. Writing with rubber gloves (embroidered, besides, with the worst of nineteenth-century embroidery). I wonder if this repugnant book has a better balance, some secret virtue, in its original German. The truth is that in Spanish it sounds like the text of *The Magic Flute* sung to the music of *Manon Lescault*.

Sidney Bechet is so emphatically corny. I like him the way I like kaleidoscopes and Utrillo's paintings.

Slight existential digression.

When I go into my "neurotic state," I spend each hour measuring my precariousness, my futility. Work is loathsome. Is it possible that work could *amuse* me? Mask of the abyss, etc . . . I fluctuate; unexpected throbs of happiness, then back to anxiety, and this two or three times a day.

So my doctor gives me some excellent drugs. Fifteen days later, if I haven't forgotten, at least I don't feel the void. I know I'm the same, but I know it like I know my seven times tables. My doctor declares me cured. The poor guy doesn't know that what he's done is *infirm me. Enfermar, enfermer.* Wadded in my vitamin shell, I pretend not to be afraid, pretend to be contented, to survive.

A friend from Mendoza tells me things about X. When Y died in an asylum, X went to identify the body. They took him into the cold storage of the morgue, opened the compartments and he could see nothing but soles of feet, one beside the other like spines of human books. A patient there knew he was looking for Y. "I know him," he said. Swiftly he chose a pair of feet and, with one tug, pulled out the corpse.

When they were leaving, X saw a ragged and dirty patient. He clutched a pigeon to his chest and caressed it continuously. He was no longer a man, he was a pigeon caress. And because this went on all the time, the pigeon's plumage was now dirty and destroyed, identical to its caress.

More on the supposed "suffering" of the writer. If you really have to suffer, let it be not for what you write but how.

What I should study is whether, when I think I've found the right road, what's actually happened is that I've lost all the rest.

If I could set out opposing themes, the ones I frown upon—Bovary vs. Flaubert *genre*. But I give up after ten pages, the thing doesn't work. I need the nearness of the lived experience, this chronicle. Although it relates nothing that moves me, I require complete possession of the theme: I belong to the ominous species of those who write when they can.

The idiocy of saying: "I have little time at my disposal—" when it is time who disposes sooner or later of you.

Those guys who snatch up the phone when it rings and shout: "Who d'ya wanna talk to, buddy?"

Malraux, *La Musée Imaginaire:*
"*. . . un style est ce par quoi un système de formes organisées que se refusent à l'imitation, peut exister en face des choses comme une autre Création.*"

Mental cankers. Each time the *langue de l'association* touches them, they hurt.

I saw Clara, from a distance, walking with a book in her hand and looking pleased.

Return of that former happiness, when we were classmates at the Faculty—No, nothing goes back to how it was. If I think I'm happy like back then,

but then no one thought in terms of comparison; we were happy with the intensity of being it, nothing more than being it. We didn't even know anything. Or we did, but it was like knowing it was hot or raining.

I can't help feeling that if dreams dispense with waking logic, or alter it, then that order doesn't belong to reality, it's just a daytime classification. Perhaps we dream noumenon, and relapse into phenomenon when we wake up. The world awaits its discoverer.

(Perchance a man at once Kant and Lautréamont—)

Poets' conversation.

The reader is a bridge, present and overhearing their dialogue. La penultième gets up to its old tricks in such disparate and distant works.

Marechal:

Suffering is born with the number two.

And from way over on the other side, César Vallejo:

With so many twos, ay, you're so alone!

When they talk to me of Giono, I am.

Angelic creatures of the YMCA! I go to have lunch and find this inscription at the entrance (they renew them every week):

I shall pass through this world but once. Any kind word that I might utter or any good that I can do, let me do it NOW. Let me not defer or neglect it, for I shall not pass this way again

Adiós appetite, farewell flat little omelette and big scallion flan. The memento is all very well, you have to sit near it and ponder it, reading it over and over again (it's been printed in the style of an optician's office). Why does that tiny hand close in my stomach? Nothing new there, the two most important points of the "thought" are topical: I shall die, *for good and ever.*

If I can be good,
be it now.

But can I be good if I'm going to die? Does not the certainty of death contradict and unravel all morality? Being good is always *forgetting something*, believing the fiesta is going to last.

This is not cynicism, given that not being good consists of numerous states without necessarily arriving at evil. What I'm trying to say is that the certainty of death does not contribute, as the YMCA wishes it would, to me embracing you and saying lofty things. He who truly knows he's going to die is not up for bullshit.

(Of course all this, seen from a religious angle—But religions falsify the problem from the start, because their raison d'être is to *alter* death. At least the little sign I read alludes quite clearly to death, to that-which-occurs-in-a-bed.)

The literary machine. How does the desire for an absolute creation reappear, with no possible error, the agreement between an idea and its judgement, a feeling and its image, a will and its projection and praxis. Literature results from a combination of heterogenesis in the making and heterogenesis in action. Just one of the operations is already a superhuman task. That is perhaps why the writer continues.

Poetry wants to be metaphysics and sometimes achieves it with Lamartine or Valéry. English poetry does it without trying, it emerges on the metaphysical level, which is its firmament and its grace.

Where Mallarmé arrives with his last exhausting wingbeat, Shelley is already naturally up there like a treetop. There is nothing restrictive in this differentiation I amuse myself with pointing out. In essence the achievements are no different; but the French poem emerges from the forge like the diamond from the stone cutter; the English verse shines with that ease we admire in the fish, or in the tennis player who returns a shot almost without moving.

Middleton Murry wears himself out attempting to explain Keats through his poems and correspondence. The usual, insurmountable mistake: forgetting that those are scraps of the great silent storm, of the windless hurricane that happens *in the intervals.*

Joyce could have not written *Portrait of the Artist*—We already had *Une saison en enfer*, which contained it in its vigorous virtuality.

Perhaps it hasn't been said that Stephen's path is the same—except in reverse—as Saint Augustine's.

Joyce doesn't write *well*; this is the merit and efficiency of a book that tries to fix a stage where there is more babbling than word, more sentiment than expression. Graham Greene put it very well in *The Ministry of Fear:* "My brother has the ideas but I feel them." Except Joyce, instead of the almost discursive definition, takes advantage of his own magnificent narrative clumsiness and gives us a book where what's felt exceeds what's said, an infrequent proportion in the profession.

Narrative clumsiness: when he *wants*. But understand that the clumsy passages (Stephen and Cranly, Stephen and Temple) are the truly great ones. I reread the Jesuit's elaborate speeches without pleasure. That hell is too good.

It's obvious that we are first *oneness* and only later—oh intelligence, magnificent bitch—comes fragmentation. From the whole to the parts, as old Parmenides liked it, hence *Gestalt*.

Ars Poetica. Almost inevitable error in poetic theorizing: to gradually approach an ever more ideal conception of the poetic act, to conceive it as supreme expression, effusion of the sublime, apex, et cetera. Such as Bremond, Valéry, Shelley.

The poet, seen from this angle, seems to be a miraculous being who arrives at the poem in a superhuman, exceptional state. We don't believe it impossible. But we recognize its infrequency, the certain fact that a great poet doesn't even need that metaphysical, rational or emotional mise en scène.

That's why Rimbaud's PontiusPilatism is still admirable: *Si le cuivre séveille clarion, C'EST PAS MA FAUTE.*

Read *Sartor Resartus.* It's no longer tolerable. There is not a single passage—not even the shuffling of symbols and silence—still fresh or meaningful. That abject adoration of the work of man—

What suits man is to create, and sniff at the created as breath for the new work. By Carlyle's route one arrives at the blessed idolatry of Progress.

Where is Carlyle's pessimism? It's not by swearing à la Manfred that one asserts a pessimism (not even a nihilism). Behind the "eternal No," this mediocre Brit hides a puerile teleological hope, a finality without a single guarantee.

Sartre, Marx, the individual and society.
They detest Sartre's "reactionary individualism." They find it

horrible that one of his heroes should "run aground in a chair" instead of going to fight in Spain. They remain blind to any salvation through the individual, perched up in the capital . . . of humanity. By way of the species one will go to the man, their creed. But no, imbeciles, only via the man. The species does not exist; it's a comfortable concept to designate associated individuals.

Clarify the notion of the "individual." As the first thing to note, this absolute: if the "individual in its pure state" (Du Bos) can truly be conceived, his conscience would *oblige* him—in order not to betray himself as a man—to shy away from all participation in a progress not his own.

To give something of oneself to others (poetry, TNT, kisses) is to recognize the integration of the *I* in the *you*. All self-denial, in that sense, is being less-man, less-self. To depend on . . . from a rigidly human individual criterion, the being-in-you (Gabriel Marcel) admits this devaluation.

The adventitious factors, procurers . . .

a) Material orders: *besoin, wants.*

b) The cowardly feeling (if only one could do another good for oneself!)

And through non-human agents, the individual succumbs gladly to the soft mattress called society. That's why every communist theory is *indignant* at heart.

Vocabularies. If you go into the "Shorthorn Grill" and order "a flat one," the waiter gives you a stupefied look. Half a block away, in the cafeteria of the YMCA, they immediately bring you an omelette.

Memory of a long-ago nocturnal escapade, with classmates from normal school. Heat, a storm. There were six or seven of us, we filled the streetcars with the name of Pirandello, *Emperor Jones*, *Petroushka*. It was 1935. We were wandering aimlessly around the Costanera, enjoying the walk, each others' presence, jokes, affection. We went into Puerto Nuevo and came to a point where the swollen river lapped within arm's reach. Then (but this should be told by Malaparte, who used to exaggerate it à la Caruso) someone shouted, and in the night we leaned over the breakwater. The river was pale and dense, and it smelled. Things like sticks, like white slippers, moved around down there. The ichthyologist of the group (because we had an ichthyologist, I swear) said: "They're dead fish." It was more than that, it was the river's vomit, a monstrous defecation that was rising towards the land, sticking to the bank . . . Further out, the water turned into its usual *café con leche* color; death was this rejection, this land's end, fetid and sickly sweet strip of dead fish, belly-up that crowded together in the night to storm Buenos Aires.

"What a night for a suicide," said the comedian. And I thought perhaps the suicides were the fish. Fish of the bank, of land, infected by the city, little catfish of the arcades who kill themselves for not getting there (or perhaps on their way back, but this is turning into a tango and I don't know, *honest injun*, if I thought of it that night).

Thinking of a monk during the decline of the Roman Empire, in some far-flung border province, alone, with dogs and images, and who would have left written testimony of the rumors he heard filtered down through the years, the rivers, the men. "One learned that a powerful king, chief of hordes, came down from the hills that lead to the sweet valleys of the center." Maybe, years later: "They say the waters of a river were diverted to bury the leader, then diverted back to their natural bed, forever hiding him from sacrilege and profane curiosity—"

I've been that monk a little, and I can imagine it clearly. From this austral tower I've heard the voices of time. They begin to fall into order, to gain height, situate themselves in profundity. Once the paper's folded and ready, it moves imperceptibly on the desk; it's alive, it has will; the swan tucks in his wings, the elephant adjusts his trunk and the rhythm of his feet: the folded paper prepares for its brief eternity as bibelot. The bouquet of flowers too; I decided to arrange a delicate bouquet, what Oscar Wilde calls a *subtle symphonic arrangement of exotic flowers*, and to see mysterious transformations, displacements, antipathies and passions of that long dead silence in operation.

I've heard things, so many. As Juan would say—regretfully—I've only heard them. Argentina's an enormous open ear. *All-America Cables.* I understand the magic prestige of names heralding messengers: Reuters, Havas, United Press. Like in *Alice*, the footman is a fish, he comes from the oceanic waters with rumors of what's happening in places where news has importance and implications. I remember: "We shall fight on the streets and in the hills . . ." I remember: "Paul Valéry has just died—" I remember: "The Negro pulverized the pure aria . . ." I remember: "They tied the moribund Laval to the post . . ." I remember (I was in a train, sitting on the left-hand side; I opened the newspaper and): "Rudolf Hess parachutes into England."

As a boy I only read about sports, crimes, and heroic feats. The headlines always in big letters. By radio—crystal set, with telephones—Firpo's *knockout.* But the next day *La Nación*, magnifying the shame: *Jack Dempsey retains heavyweight championship of the world.* And years later (on the platform in the station, *El Mundo*): *He lost but put up a great fight* (Justo Suárez vs. Billy Petrolle). Further back, further back . . . Saint-Martin, an aviator (a few lines by Fernández Moreno [?] in *Caras y Carretas* [?]: "The shadow of Saint-Martin / floating over the waters"), De Pinedo, Jim Mollison.

Johnny Weissmuller, Joe Choynsky's remembrances in *La Nación*, the photographs of Bob Fitzsimmons with his speckled skin and the corkscrew punch to the solar plexus. I explained to my mother: "See how he hits twisting his arm, so that . . ." Lindbergh!

(I vaguely see titles, hear conversations: the Ruhr, coal . . .)

To think they have this picture here, today, people who later vote (but I'm thinking this in the name of Juan, aristocratic socialist poet).

If I remembered (or invented) the monk, it was for other reasons. There comes a day when the ear achieves its education, when the snail learns to distinguish sounds. It's very sad not to have any personal destiny except not to have one, but in an emergency one can at least be a good ear, an ear that understands the tonality and atonalities of his times. If Theseus of Cuverville says: *I lived*, the monk murmurs in Buenos Aires, *I heard*. There even comes a day when one learns to listen, to disdain mere sounds.

Thirty years at this pace is a long concert. I don't lament my thirty-year-long audition, I think they've contained more, in every sense, than the thirty preceding years. I was born in the first month of the first war, in a city occupied by von Kluck's forces. When I began to properly hear what got as far as Buenos Aires, it was the end of silent film, Mussolini, Romain Rolland, the sinking of the Mafalda, Cocteau, Milosz, the 6th of September, Uriburu, the

Civic Legion, Hitler, *I am a Fugitive from a Chain Gang*, Federico, Michaux, *Sur*, Klemperer, the extension of Corrientes (vague recollection of its "realist" cinemas in long, long halls, with blurry films where satyrs with bangs and tough necks chased poor stupid young girls through apartments absolutely filled with *bric-à-brac*, Lacroze subway, the wonder of escalators, expedition of discovery with fourth grade classmates, the stretch of Canning Dorrego, the vertigo of Maldonado's paunch . . . The *Graf Zeppelin*, Gene Tunney, Gertrude Ederle, Ramón Novarro, Tito Schipa, Lily Pons, the Prince of Wales, Roura . . .

And later, I don't know, reading, love, the end of school, music (Stravinsky, the unforgettable night of *Symphony of Psalms*), plazas, cafés—

But this is already contact, coexistence. I truly begin at this point. I begin in front of Don Segundo Sombra, crying; in front of the dazzle—it was in 1937—of an issue of Nosotros and there, casual as you like, the sonnets of *Death in the Pampas:*

> How the icy air must smother you
> over your pale mouth, my torment
> dormant—

The ear kept hearing, but the voice was wind now, softness of a caressing feather, proximity.

Regarding liberty and the free being:

They say: "Heifetz does what he wants with his violin." Isn't it the violin that does what it wants with Heifetz?

This is a piano, given and immutable. The boy who wants to become a pianist has clumsy hands (but clumsy always means availability, starting point of innumerable paths; to be clumsy is to be free); pliable hands, the antithesis of the keyboard that laughs at them with all its teeth.

Gradus ad Parnassum, Czerny, arpeggios—technique. But the piano doesn't change, it confines itself to moulding the man, making him into a pianist, a piano-man, a servant in black livery who travels the world. Free hands turn into hands adept *for* . . . (A hammer, a cigarette paper—otherworldly problems; the pianist's hand belongs ever more to the piano and ever less to the man.)

All this is not a defense of the uselessly clumsy and free (freely useless) but it intrigues me as a prejudice-washing sponge. Watch out, Andrés, for so-called liberties that are nothing but the perfection of the delivery.

I see the concert this way: the violin makes Heifetz carry it, and rests on the chin and hand of its servant. Adapting himself strictly to the will of his master, the servant performs the necessary movements so the violin will sound. The little freedom left to Heifetz, mechanically tied to his tyrant, is dissolved in the worst sort of slavery to the dead tyrants, the three Bs, the mysterious Italian, Falla's jota, the fountain of Arethusa thusa caricathusa.

A *mot* worth remembering, spoken by Norah Borges at a very formal luncheon, when the enormous tureen of stew was set upon the table:
— How looovely! It looks like sewage!

The anecdote, *le mot*, illuminates with a brief sparkle brighter than any description. The French and English critics know it, and since the seventeenth century the fixing of these key phrases has been an important task. If I hung around with writers, I'd write down every witticism that seemed meaningful — not the mere ingenious games; and I'd be doing a good turn for the poor biographers of 1995. We are so neglected here; how will they ever reconstruct Molinari's entourage one day? Years ago they at least practiced reportage, which helped to fix anecdotal elements; today, with no newspapers, no magazines, no desire to know ourselves: We leave behind nothing but books and letters, things we've thought through; even the photographs that preserve a profile, a chin, we have taken by Saderman.

If painters did more portraits of writers (or among themselves) we would have the *mot plastique*. Sergio Sergi says more about Daniel Devoto and Alberto Dáneo than any possible future biographies. He told me—and his phrase is his portrait—: "It won't do, you've got a bland face; your expressions are in your hands."

(One of Sergio the bear's jokes when signing a drawing: S.S.S. S.S. [*su seguro servidor* = your humble servant])

In *Correo Literario*, Ulyses Petit de Murat wrote a story about the *Martín Fierro* group; he saw the necessity for personal memories in filling out the due homage, and his references to Borges are tinted with substance that will later defend biographers from lies, sterilization or reconstruction based on conjecture. I found a splendid Borges *mot* there, grabbing Petit de Murat by the lapels when he agreed with him about something, and saying:

—And who do you think you are, you little pipsqueak, not to contradict me?

(I quote from memory.)

The fact, as always, precedes the explanation, which in any case does nothing but surround it, name it and reassure our conceptual control. Before understanding with sufficient dialectic clarity the irruption of poetry in any contemporary verbal genre, and by extension the eradication of "genres" as such, I felt its obscure work present in my prose, in what up till then had been prose. I wrote a novel where, without excessive effort, I managed to express well and clearly a repertoire of ideas and a set of sensations and sentiments. Later, amusing myself with a few short stories, I noticed the first signs of rot in that prose; fear of the "emphatic" period, the *"fortissimo"* end of chapter. Every proposition that contains a whole development of its object, is like a tiny chapter, and *ergo* should finish "roundly"; a discourse—and my prose was always discourse, like this that I write now effortlessly, because its content is rigorously transmissible—is composed of dozens of propositions, each one of which has its progression, its peripeteia, its knot and its final crash, that *artistic* order that masters emotion and moves to applause, a gesture that consists of hitting the hands together to see if one can trap in them the *je ne sais quoi* that provokes enthusiasm.

When I realized I could no longer write like before, that language had turned its back on me, that the *rhythms* were demanding otherwise, and that on the whole what I was now writing (because

I didn't for a single minute decline the entreaty from within) was less valuable as *meaning* than as *object*, I had the first suspicion of the contemporary phenomenon. That was when I read *Ulysses*, with a South American delay. And I confirmed what was happening when I accidentally stumbled upon *The Death of Virgil*.

Bitter maté. Distraction. *Somebody loves me* — Dinah Shore's sweet voice. It bores me to explain. Indolence. And this is another proof of what I'm trying to say. To explain is always to define a fact, an object, a system of ideas, a conviction, a confirmation. Precisely what I've left behind. I now feel that nothing is of interest as explanation; the explanation is barely of interest because it brings the fact back to us and us to the fact, the object, et cetera. Horror of influences. A chain: So-and-so loves a book about Cézanne because he likes Cézanne, who liked painting. How far from painting So-and-so ends up! Or this: there is a sacred horror, Keats writes *Hyperion* because *Hyperion* is his sacred horror. Middleton Murry becomes interested in Keats because he's attracted by *Hyperion;* I read Middleton Murry because I like Keats. But there is a sacred horror and it ain't Middleton Murry.

As I was saying, the first thing I noticed were the changes in verbal rhythm. Farewell prosody. It began slowly, commas that didn't fall into place. I'd always liked the semicolon: suddenly disgust, impossibility of using it. I remember when correcting exams written by students of a state secondary school, I was annoyed by their inability to perceive the moment when the verbal structure finished, and how the intermediate punctuation marks (comma, colon, semicolon, dashes) helps to disconnect while connecting, shows that you have to leave one room to enter another. I was irritated by things like: "Joan of Arc set off for Orléans, the English troops had conquered a great deal of territory . . ." That strange ignorance of the so useful, so clear function of the semicolon. Suddenly I felt the need to let the clauses overlap, gallop together over the weak bridge of the comma, or be set entirely loose and free. Let the prose surge like a swell. In chains of adjectives, demand for liberty: "Suddenly alone fed up furious so prudent, oh poor woman." And this arising from the ruins of my past fastidiousness, joyfully paining me. A feeling of liberty, of fair play, of rhetorical non-conviction, of *demonstration* and no longer of *description*.

"You, who used to write so well . . ." a woman once said to me.

Stages: after finishing with the arrangement of punctuation (not me, it finishes itself off), the need to substitute more and more often the trapping of an "idea," its conception, by the material in its given form—what they wrongly call "crude." But this broke the horizontality of the writing (which is the spatializing of temporal development). When, during a carnival, it occurred to me to write a short story and flying to the typewriter, the impulse to express the blocks of material (and this was already total submission to the mechanics – ! – of poetry, to the form in which it irrupts and is given) led me

to this

to undo the successive horizontality

(it's not new, I know; but it's new to me)

and in a splattering leap, sprinkling on the paper what was really the tail swish of a wave, a global experience.

In other words what Mallarmé understood, what Guillaume and Pierre Reverdy did. But I *narrated*. That's why the staves still mark the trail. I jump when there's a need, and if everything is finally poetry, my poem tells, that is it shows a face, an act, it goes down the street, speaks voices, dialogues, shows thoughts,

without tying itself to anything that turns it into *reflection*, instrument, symbolic mise-en-scène operation.

Ay, language is our original sin. *Moi, esclave de mon langage.* Always, in itself, reflection and instrument. But liberty, won by the putrefaction of my excellent former prose, lies in getting as close as possible to the material to be expressed, the physical or fictitious material I want (or I'm obliged) to express. For this I escape from *adequate* language (which it isn't anyway, more like adequating) and I accept, provoke, invent and try out a way of saying things that—me keeping quite still in the middle—is a self-asserting of all that surrounds me, interests me, and awakens me. There you are, memory of a night on Congreso, an adolescent weeping on a bench. You are there, it's you. Well, now it's your turn because I want it to be, or because I accept that you want it: come, *say yourself.* This is a hand, this is a sheet of paper. Pass through me like light through a stained-glass window: make yourself word, be here. The order of the elements doesn't matter, it doesn't matter if you're really stained glass and the word illuminates you, making you be, or if you are the light itself and my word (yours, yes, but mine) will be little by little the stained glass that gives you meaning forever.

For others, which is the miracle.

I read, in Apollinaire, this that goes so well with my childhood: *"Je ne sais pourquoi je l'avais appelé Maldino. Je forgeais des noms pour toutes les choses qui me frappaient. Une fois, je vis un poisson sur le table de la cuisine. J'y pensais longtemps, me le désignant du nom de Bionoulour."* *(Giovanni Moroni)*

I already suspected, as a boy, that naming something was to make it mine. That wasn't enough, though, I always needed to periodically change the names of those around me, because that way I was rejecting conformity, the slow substitution of a being by a name. One day I would begin to feel that the name wasn't going well anymore, it was no longer the thing it named. The thing was there, shiny and new, but the name had worn out like a suit. By giving it a new denomination, I obscurely proved to myself that what mattered was the other thing, that reason for my name. And for weeks the thing or the animal or the person would appear beautiful to me beneath the light of its new sign.

There was a cat I loved so much he had four names during his brief life (he was poisoned with the cyanide my grandmother put down the anthills); one was the common one, what everybody called him, and the others secret, for private conversations. A dog the clan called *Míster* I called *Mistirto*, and it was important because I'd just read Michel Zévaco's *Nostradamus* and the character Myrtô was hanging around. That was how I could objectify him magically, and *Mistirto* was much more than a dog.

And you have to remember, way back, the beautiful animal with its white fur I found to call you, and how you liked to imitate it with a caress, with modesty, with pure shamelessness.

Phrase:

    —I find it hard to believe. It's as if they told me that ivory comes from an animal.

Anti-poem to rouse to fury.

The Egyptians embalmed their mothers
with fishes' tears and linen *passe-partout*
to take them to the hypogea
on a special reserved streetcar, which
is an eminently Egyptian
machine.

Stupid things they say: "If it were within my power, I would never permit this or that."

    It's possible, if the power was given to you now, miraculously. But if you'd grown up enclosed in your power, slave of your power, you'd be on the side of the ones who do the beating.

I pick up the receiver to make a call. Before I can dial the number, a voice speaks to me. The dialogue goes more or less like this:

—Hello.

—Hello.

—With whom do you wish to speak, sir?

—With whom do *you* wish to speak?

—Look, I hadn't had time to dial the number when I heard your voice.

—Oh, the lines are crossed.

—Please hang up.

Later, when there's nothing but silence, I wonder *who* that man is. *Where* is he, what's the room he's speaking from like. We intersected for three seconds and got to know each others' voices. And we had nothing to say to each other, we spoke by *mistake*.

I suddenly feel so close to him.

Theme for the cruelest, truest novel: someone loves, hopelessly but taking pleasure in the joy of contemplating her youthful perfection. Years of absence go by, and he returns. Then that creature appears, with a friendly smile. It's her, but she's changed. Now she's fixed in her limit, in her clearly defined personality. The beholder —who thought he still loved her—discovers he only loves the echo of her former self, which she does not remember, which she squandered through her life.

The cruelty of that confrontation, of that terrible comparison.

Now Morgan, in *Portrait in a Mirror*—But Nigel and Clara at least manage to embrace, even though they're looking for their other phantoms. Here there was nothing but games of images in parallel mirrors.

Or that marvellous incarnation of the unattainable that David Lichine gives in *L'après-midi d'un faune*, dancing on another plane from the nymphs, separated from them by a fine, inviolable wall of air.

Vagus quidam, as Petrarch said of a disciple. I'm reading Suetonius, Tacitus, Ellery Queen—

Half-asleep phrase: *With a distant sound of menopause and eider-downs*—

Everything about that man was small and provincial. He led a *narrow-gauge* life.

Be careful of realism when writing. Avoid zoological fauna, summon up unicorns and tritons and give them *reality*. Literature, as Malraux says of the plastic arts, should have an independent creation, where the everyday world has as much influence as the writer will tolerate, and no more.

Clara can say, like Judith in *Dusty Answer:* "But I can't live in ugliness."

Without her being entirely aware if it, the contours of her life are gradually closing over her and over Juan. They would be surprised if I told them, they know they're such *porteños,* so much their milieu—

What they haven't seen yet is that they're carrying on, but the milieu, little by little, is being taken away from them. Like an imperceptible removal, a house that loses its furniture piece by piece, its curtains, its paintings, while the life of its inhabitants continues with no possible variation.

A short story that illustrated this gradual dispossession wouldn't be bad; how the people, without noticing, are left without chairs, without books, records, images, sheets—

Petit homage à Radiguet:

He wrote novels where the alleged grand human themes were ignored. He was of the opinion that the future belonged to the louts and no one would write for minorities anymore. He then hastened to secure a good position in the oblivion of posterity; he considered it his duty.

Terrible land of dreams, where the law is a kaleidoscope. One whole night I inhabited the face, the body, the tenderness of someone dear to me, whom I meet in the street or in so many mutually appreciated places. This person also returns in the next dream; governing my sleep for weeks with the same cold petulance as in life.

Then it ceases. The image of this person has popped into my head so many times while walking down the street, into a café, in front of poems we'd once both liked. I touch with these hands the same region daily; nothing changes in this continuous celebration of a discouragement. But then, abruptly, it's gone. I dream marvelous episodes for a whole night where that person's presence would be necessary, almost imperative. They're not there. Even dreaming I'm aware of it. I know when I wake up that I won't see their image again for weeks; the kaleidoscope has been slightly turned, and other laws regulate this world in which only one common element persists: my eye that looks and looks.

A *Journal* like Gide's, entirely awake, without a yawn. Oh, this notebook is a cage full of monsters; and outside is Buenos Aires.

Flowers have all exquisite figures. (Bacon)

I extract this delicious quote from my *Webster's*. It's worth reading the twenty-three paragraphs devoted to *figure*. Few things can feed the imagination like a good dictionary. One draws one's own conclusions, there is no fear or suspicion that they might be trying to "win you over (heart and mind)" — stupid expression.

A low, white, translucent sky, so hard up against me that if I turn my head I feel it in my hair, in my ears. It's not the sky, it's the sheet on my summer bed. I'm ten years old and traveling inside my bed.

Secret delight of the encounter with my body, its geography beneath the milky light, beneath the fragrant heat. Covered by the sheet, curling up in a ball little by little to advance with the precaution of an *amateur* towards the most central and most hidden; accepting that reality entirely my own (and not creating it, it's a lie that the child creates his world in so much as creating supposes conscious creation; the child creates his world the way a tree creates its leaves). Then breaking away from the small miseries of convalescence, remembering or expecting medicines, missing school, the vague horror of all one should do and all that's threatened. Alone, in his tiny, bright kingdom, beneath his petulant wakefulness, the boy enters the perfect voyage, star-guided adventures recorded in fine logbooks.

There was a hostile but strangely conciliatory space there, where dangers didn't really threaten although their presence demanded struggle, the wise eye calculating, the sudden swipe at circumstance. Two warriors were walking with the boy and went ahead clearing a trail, sending out scouts; his hands grew in the interior landscape, stained with mossy shadows (my green pajamas!), and suddenly independent of formal tasks, of being nothing more than hands. Spiders, tents, fat Lansquenets, microscopic little horses, the two came and went deliciously, and the boy invented wars for his double army: hand-to-hand combat that lasted hours (hours of sheet as sky, because I had my time, my light and my will there). Or they didn't wage war, simply Burke, Stanley, pale Shackleton —I always thought of Shackleton as pale and Nansen enormous —and my servile corps, still and clumsy, from Niger, Victoria Nyanza, Spitzburg; gulf and cove, you could get lost in the half-light beyond the knees, jungle for one last effort, bent over to arrive, suffocating, at the *terra incognita* of my world, at the whitish isthmus of my skinny little ankles.

Mythology of the bed, with its *Jabberwockies* and moon-dwellers. Without really knowing, I had the impression that my sheet saved me from a reality just as full of delights but suddenly menaced by blunders, sad duties, embarrassments, by the atrocious servitude of childhood in the hands of affection and education. Like a giant clear eyelid, I had only to close the sheet over so much desolate sensibility to feel free, on my way to a dream more beautiful than dreaming because it could be invented and directed. Now

I suspect that my games were oneiric, that the best of their lights, their deeds and adventures were achieved by the same invention that illuminates dreams worth remembering. (As an adult, when I dreamed the story of Banto—which I've recounted somewhere or other—the scene of the tropical forest had the same rather liquid qualities of fish tank vegetation that my pajamas, my half-closed eyes, the rosy gray light of the sheet gave off, and the heat was that body heat that smells of washcloth, of thirty-seven point four degrees and Vicks VapoRub, of all the remedies for asthma, bronchitis, and the Banto—a bug, a dreamed-up insect—was like one of my hands, those things that wandered through my world and brought me news and reports.)

After twelve years, I attend a second Brailowsky concert. With some sadness—not too much—I find he's been abandoned by music, and only the piano remains faithful to him.

I was arriving at Chacarita to catch the subway when I saw a little white dog die. The car swerved with its front wheels but caught him with one of the others. In that second (in which the bare event occurs with such a pure oneiric quality that people say: "It seemed like a dream") the elements of what happened dissociated strangely. The sight and sound reached me separately, like apprehensions that weren't linked. The sound was like a ball banging hard against a wall, a loud, sharp *plop;* the sight was a prodigious *ralenti:* the dog was on his side, with two paws up in the air and his mouth open for a bark he didn't manage to voice. Slowly (this was unending) he was twisting until he rested on his side on the ground. I think he was dead from the start, although he still had organic life for a while; his inexpressiveness proved it, that slow movement that was just the effect of gravity, a remainder of the crash taking its time through his body.

August 17

A century since the death of San Martín, the mysterious. No one knew or knows who went under that name. He was strolling along the pulsing nocturnal sidewalk, and when we see him it's just in passing at corners, when he lights his cigarette under a streetlamp. He wears his poncho pulled up to his eyes, lowers it for barely an instant; maybe, if we snatched away his poncho, he would no longer be under it.

I remember: he had his back to me, sweating, devastated. He moaned slowly, with abrupt tremors that exasperated me with an excess of piety, a piety that ended in rage at seeing him so defeated, so quietly surrendered.

I washed his face with cotton and alcohol, I sat him up, refreshing his wrists and fingers, massaging his arms. Now he moaned less, regarded me affectionately, his hair falling over his forehead. I combed his hair, made him comfortable among the pillows. He smelled of bitter sweat, of the onset of dirtiness, like rancid wax. When I brought him *café con leche* and began giving him spoonfuls, blood burst out of his nose, an unstoppable gush. I had to tilt his head back, stop it up with cotton; and the pains returned, and he was exasperated, appalled.

Later, taking advantage of my having to leave Buenos Aires for two days, he went into the worst stage of his illness and I just had time to watch him die, a night of savage white moonlight over the patio.

I repeat this all to myself because every day I hate our conditional friendships more. I don't think very many people would withstand a week of physical coexistence, carrying wet rags, mopping up vomit.

Someone says to me: "I don't find intellectual friendships acceptable." I know very well what he was trying to express. He wants friends, not colleagues. But even like that, what a distance to friendship. In Buenos Aires I could not (because I know I *should not*) arrive unexpectedly at the house of my best friend; you have to telephone first, ceremoniously. And also, you mustn't seek out the same friend two days in a row—that's why we have three or four and they take turns, and we take turns—; the second visit would probably be boring. Barely changing an Italian saying: *L'amico è come il pesce: dopo tre giorni, puzza.*

The second visit is boring because the first was sufficient and then some for the friendly function: *viz* to trade all the news and exchangeable opinions, to exhaust together a spectacle or music, and enjoy affection by seeing each other. Like run-down batteries, you have to wait four or five days for the voltage to return. "How great to see you!" Discretion is what we call the skillful staging of indifference here. It astonishes me to realize that my best friend loves me without really knowing why; because of the irrationality of affection, and personal fragments I've confided to him. The worst is that we avoid elegantly, sportingly and with great beauty, those tingling displays included in the atrocious word confidences. To think that certain key things in the life of my best friend, I know third-hand. And here we graze the sphere of specialization: it's not strange that we fearlessly tell another (not at all intimate) something we keep from our friend. There is one shelf for hats and another for underpants.

I don't put much faith in those who start calling you mate after ten minutes and who can be mating with a woman after two hours. I don't believe in confidences, in verbal sexuality over cocktails.

I've proof that it's worth less than our noble technique of water-tight compartments.

It just hurts to substantiate, in the midst of good company, so many insuperable islands.

(In the afternoon) Re-read the previous. Basically, *too sexy*.

And also (or consequently) this *Heilt du bist so schön* that every day seems to me more *du was*, this Peter Pan of puppet theater, this return, like in recurring dreams, to the same house (but it's no longer—understand this—the same!) and to the same beings (not even their faces are left, idiot, they wear their hair differently now, speak with words full of cynical security, each one in his métier, well up-to-date, their own date).

It's senseless, *that's how it is*. With innuendoes, barely perceptible nuances. I persist in retaining my earliest childhood, the contents of which sufficed then and distress me now in a backlash; and at the same time, in so many ways, I am with my present now, in my inevitable age: I advance with my generation, I share and am my generation in its defeat—monstrous defeat of the generation of thirty-five; I get along well with its special fetishes and key words.

(And while that's happening, I am not with it. I am sitting in Plaza

Once—not in Plaza Miserere—and I'm reading Panait Istrati, not Jean Genêt who I'm actually reading.)

Worse still. It always happens that at a certain moment a generation tries to equate itself with its predecessors. If in 1935 I wouldn't have dared approach Martínez Estrada, in 1947 I walked at his side and was able to be a not-too-unworthy interlocutor. Now my generation lunches, talks and writes in the same circles as Mallea, Borges, Victoria and Molinari. Tomorrow, the kids who leave the high school this afternoon, exchanging punches, enthusiasm and puppyish tenderness, will come to us as equals.

On my bench in the Plaza Once I would ponder those I've mentioned. It was 1936. I thought of them, distant masters. I thought of Molinari, of Borges.

I'd like to be on my bench in the Plaza Once thinking of them now.

Music for this idiotic way I am: *Gonna take a sentimental journey* —(whining, and pronounced *seniménal*).

I suppose the reason—among others—is that I couldn't overcome the marvel of the years around 1936. When I emerged from them, it was the plain of the south, then of the west; I let myself get into a routine, the nightly cultivation of memory. Enveloped in tobacco, in *caña seca*, bitter *maté*, I kept hearing the sonata in A by César Franck day after day, I kept reading: *"Jadis si je me souviens bien—"* *Et je me souvenais.*

Martínez Estrada gives a lecture on Balzac, and in the hall of the Sociedad Científica Argentina this exemplary phenomenon takes place: the lecturer is in front of the audience, but a speaker system projects his voice from the back of the hall, so we get it in the nape of our necks. A microphone and horizontal lampshade are interposed between our eyes and the lecturer's face, disfiguring it.

But since the cinema and records have habituated us to these decompositions of a man into his constituent parts, we remain calm before this monstrous divorce, which projects over us the image of a disfigured face, speaking without being heard; and a voice coming separately, from the opposite direction, a soundtrack that (gratuitous but alarming suspicion) is possibly not the voice of the lecturer, but dubbing.

Make a character in a short story or novel say:

—*In general* I distract myself from the voice by writing what I desire to see perpetuated; I don't know any other action nor any other way of integration. I suspect I am (like so many others) the guilty conscience of the void, the *étonnement* of nothingness. Or I create the void, I gradually generate it around me.

(and it's a silly and inane void that's valid only for me)

In one way or another, I go against it, I tilt against its airy blades. But I know that's how it wants it to be, me holding out

until one day when I'm no longer useful to it, when my strength gives way.

I can foresee that day, as Cyril Connolly foresaw it so well: the symptom will be so clear,

this: when the despair becomes such that it no longer spurs on creation.

The wind of space will come in through the open window, for no one.

In the order of obligations, of work, it's good for me to be subjected to having to earn a salary (I would never say, even when distracted: "earn a living"); the fatigue of that impersonal work pitches me all the more enthusiastically into reading, a concert, an ardent pursuit.

What really frustrates me (little man, timorous toadstool) is the work of love, of affection, of the bonds with my people. I don't lose freedom because I work, but because I work to conserve the circle, the *family reunion*, the enjoyment of friendships. I don't know how to break the ties; what's worse, I see clearly that I should break them (or at least have the certainty that I could do it tonight or next week); I detect in myself the seed of those who need to be alone to give something, but I'm still in Buenos Aires, surrounded by people who love me well—as for that, when one hasn't chosen the affection, it means . . .

It's easy to say: if what on the whole I am capable of producing is a verbal work, a book or two, the circumstances do not matter.

It's easy to think that at the moment Mallarmé was weighing words with delicate mental movements to express *la famille des iridées*, the vegetable trains were making his table tremble on the rue de Rome.

But what matters is to establish daily how the circle imposes its law, provokes reactions, polishes the edges, infects vocabularies, erodes protruding points, unifies creeds; how what we call "the group," "the gang" or "our team" (the *Sur* team, the *Colegio Libre* team . . .) resolves problems malignantly

seeing as the problem is my bull, not the group's bull, the cowardly heifer,

and enables friendly smoothings out in life

(go see Pancho so he'll give you a discount in *Albion House*)

and channels untamed destinies into well-lubricated chutes

(you have to read Greene; you have to go to the *Cine Club;* you should be the one to write the review of the Monona book . . .)
and mamá, so ill,
and the insurance policy, and

Horreur de ma bêtise. That's what it is, you so detached, you knew it. Where my little bull stays, as Juan would say, who walks alongside me—and that really is bad for both of us in this anti-gregarious rage:

If loving weren't staying,
if loving weren't heliotropic,
if loving weren't mimetic,
if staying weren't resembling
(or resembling in difference),
if resembling weren't losing oneself
or self-forgetting

Enough. I'm coming out sounding like León Felipe mixed with an antikipling *If.*
Silly antikipling, for today, this Sunday evening.
And I'm drinking this whisky for you Cyril Connolly, Palinurus, *mon semblable*

mon

   con

   frère.

Such a huge fear of winning the lottery that I buy one ticket after another to banish luck.

In front of certain people you have to play the fool to not be taken for a fool.

List of received ideas that circulate in my family:
   Never speak while eating fish.
   Never drink wine after watermelon.
   Broth is always very nutritious.
   One mustn't sleep beneath the moon.
   The only good tomato sauce is the one made at home.
   A servant used to cost twenty pesos a month and they were loyal. Now—et cetera.
   Never bathe after eating, except immediately and with hot water.
   Americans are abnormal, sickly beings because they only eat canned food.

Art:

Artists, you know what kind of life they lead, et cetera.

—A violet horse! (Typical exclamation.)

—But that painting, what does it represent?

This photograph is lovely, not just a perfect likeness but it looks just like a painting.

(Vice versa.)

Italian opera is beautiful because it is melodic, Wagner on the other hand is just shouting and noise.

This film is a drama, because it ends sadly; this other one is a dramatic comedy because it has a happy ending.

Charles Laughton and Peter Lorre are disgusting.

Politics:

Governments ought to be strong.

Those poor monarchs, losing their thrones one by one.

Children:

Children should sleep with their hands under the pillow.

Children speak when hens piss. (My great-grandmother's phrase.)

Children shall never say they don't like something.

You don't say vomit, but throw up. (Variation in Auntie's house: bring up.)

Vocabulary: popó, pipí, pitito, pepé, pajarito. (Note when the adolescent sets up his own corresponding creole vocabulary, P remains the dominant letter. Nice theme for a thesis.)

You must always eat soup, because it's the best food, etcetera.

Lots of carrots, because carrots and pumpkin help the calf muscles develop.

Children never drink wine. (On New Year's Eve, let them get wasted.)

A boy who smokes will grow up to be tubercular.

Speaking of Drieu, Victoria quotes this phrase: "I shall never allow the broader circles to hide the small ones . . ." He's alluding to mental systems, to creeds; the Tao will not hide the treaty of Versailles from him.

I think this in respect to personal life, I think of the overly famous *To see the world in a grain of sand.* Maybe what matters is to see the grain of sand as a grain of sand; to acquire an appreciation of the small, of the minor, of the—if you like—unnecessary. It's easy to love a bee when you think of it as God's receptacle, his creature; it's not so easy to love it just as a bee, grain of sand in the air.

I say to a friend: "Can you imagine at my age still being moved by a little record where there are sixteen bars that contain the great heart of a man who died and who was called Bix?" He says: "No."

I suggest: "Listen to this meditation by Coleman Hawkins." He listens, *poli et bienveillant;* the music bounces off his skin, I see it. Then, with the slightest excuse, he speaks of Chabrier, of the great and the good. I know he's got reason on his side. Nothing more than reason.

This isn't the worst case, pure *eutrapelia.* The worst is seeing how the grand ideas—democracy, morality, et cetera; fascism, power, et cetera—do not just condition the immediate circumstances of a man, but induce him to conceal it, to sacrifice the small circle to the large one. When you think of Music, it's bad for poor music.

You'll tell me (I'm writing in the style of Horace): "By way of musics one ascends to Music." Yet another reason not to forget that the staircase is made up of steps.

You could tell me something weightier: "The arrival at the summit *demands* the abandonment of the valley." But listen, mountaineer: if you deprive yourself of the solace of the valley, of its tender freshness, how do you get up to your summit? And furthermore, when you're at the summit, what's left to look at if not the valley?

Because the sky, after a while, is a drag. You have to look back at the valley. If the valley's good for anything, it's for stimulating the ascent to the summit; if the summit's good for anything, it's for *choosing*, now that everything's on view, what truly matters about the valley. And don't forget G.K.: "Only one thing is necessary: everything."

My friend says: "The small, the grain of sand . . . such vagueness of terms." So we'll clarify, always from the summit: you have (or should have) your small, and I have mine. Since we've talked about music, what you or I might like of *folk*—I won't complete the word because it stinks—the worthy minor musicians, the products of one happy hour, the improvisation held in wax, the timbre of a voice, the memory of a shanty heard on deck, among stars. And so on.

Rupert Brooke put it better than I can in *The Great Lover*. I'm with him: he's a man who's capable of carving out, beside the resounding catalogue of the ships, a tiny inventory of elytra, of pauses, looks, a whistled negro spiritual while walking beside a stream, of flavors, Colette or Nathalia Crane phrases; of names, gestures, odd lines,

and the blue of a pair of virgin eyebrows

and everything that second by second sustains life. Don't forget, swimmer, that the big wave that carries you runs over the hidden back of the sands.

Balzac—Martínez Estrada reminds me in his course—worked fourteen to eighteen hours a day. Lucky him, with the supposed unhappiness of the writer martyr (blah blah) enduring such stretches.

I'm sure he was entirely happy writing like that; that's what his life was for, and excursions were only something like changing the water in the goldfish bowl, preparing his eyes and his heart for the attack where Rastignac impatiently awaited him.

I envy the capacity for work that ruins Balzac's health, but at the same time demonstrates it. I am never so happy now as when I'm alone in front of my notebook. Why, then, after writing for two hours, do I start having hyperaesthesia, tachycardia, claustrophobia, nausea. Feeling obliged to leave it all—but I wanted to finish one chapter, it's so much fun—phone a friend, open my door, accept the interruption of lunch, the newscast, the radio.

It's tempting to explain this by a split personality. I know how much I suffer writing, corroborating with each new sentence how imperfect and futile was the last; that horrible comparison with the Idea awaiting (bah, I'm the one who waits) its actualization. And nevertheless my suffering is this continuous pleasure of returning to the task. Why does it eventually defeat me? That is: why does the pulse, that pressure gauge of a little motor, react to the negative aspects and not to the profound pleasure of my work? Cardiac neurosis that plays its dirty tricks—and not just with work; stopping the party like the sailor with his albatross collar, to say: "You're too happy, come on over here to suffer awhile." Stella advises me: "Go see a psychoanalyst." That's how we are these days, in the total unease that this uncultured civilization creates in so many beings: when the Genie fails one has to see a psychoanalyst. Look, Stella, it's a subtle and insidious thing, the intelligence suffers at work, the artistic part, but the central part that matters is delighted because I'm obeying, because I write nothing that is not born of a necessity rather than an interest. This absurd organic fatigue only proves my incapacity as conductor, the interferences and censorship of the mental plane. My prose is a memory of the dead, injured and survivors of this battle

where ignorant armies clash by night

as Matthew Arnold says; battle of elements against categories, of things against their presumed names, of shadows and objects that slip out escaping from the truthful mouth of their concepts. And I get the blame.

The only thing to do is leave. Staying is already the lie, the construction, the walls that parcel up the space but don't nullify it.

Suddenly, standing in the middle of a room, the discovery that I'm only in it because I *want* to be. I would only have to stretch out my hand in space, just a little. And slip into nothingness through that essential gap.

In *Men as Gods*, Wells glimpsed that area of air (but in reality it's an area of man) through which one can pass into another world. His physical vitality drove him to invent himself an *ersatz* heaven, to realize the old illusion of heaven with man in charge. I didn't know—I didn't want to know—that the gap is everywhere, but it leads nowhere.

Sometimes I think that to die is to cheat the void a little. The true annihilation should happen in life, like this: I slowly stretch out my hand, touch the void, and there I go. To die, on the other hand, is like entering into a passive nothing.

To kill yourself, happy medium: manufacture the gap.

The quintessential human gesture is staying. *I am, therefore I stay,* and vice versa. When I say "human" I don't say it affirmatively. The true legitimate, human gesture can be nothing but this: *They brought me* into the world, where I have nothing and do nothing that isn't a low reaction against my involuntary origin. There-fore—and this is where you have to start stretching out your hand, probing space like a fish probes at a fisherman's net.

The saddest idea: that the gap isn't in space but in time.

The "consolation": keep your hand ready every minute.

All I have to do is love something for a nightmare to show me an aping, its offensive travesty. I love cats so much; enough to dream—I'm still living the image—the transformation in my arms of a green-eyed cat, its face suddenly cruel, growing in size, the horrible attack on my hands, the leap towards my eyes. Strange that I thought (I felt him bite my neck, and was now in the whole horror of the nightmare): "This is what it must feel like to be killed by a (panther) (tiger)."

Very clear feeling of censorship, upon waking. The cat thing continued and closed an instantly forgotten episode. This is the link left hanging: I was in something like a telephone booth, and a woman handed me a cat under the door.

Geist des Volkes. An idiotic phrase popular here, when we want to be ironic about someone else's silliness or cynicism: *"Che, ¿vos sos o te hacés?"* [Hey, are you or do you make yourself?] I remember the origin; in a radio broadcast from Cine París (1931 or '32) Paco Busto said it several times. The phrase was: *"Dígame, usted es o se hace . . . el zonzo?"* [Tell me, are you making a fool of yourself or does it come naturally?] The pause made it comical, the fecal sense of *"hacerse"* et cetera.

Strange that Sartre comes along now and shows us that man is not, but makes himself. In all seriousness we could answer our comedian: "The truth is, *che*, I am not; I just make myself—"

The admirable thing in the "career" of a writer like Gide, is the progressive, harmonious development of the parts that will one day luxuriantly make up the tree blowing in the breeze. The contradictions, searching, rebellion and encounters of the first books; the "stages," the fixations, the organization of sensory, intellectual and moral systems around notions and experiences *proved upon the pulses* as Keats put it. To gradually notice, while reading his oeuvre chronologically, how becoming a writer (I give the word all its human significance) has less to do with writing certain things than with resigning oneself and deciding not to write many others. Since he can't go back over Michel, Ménalque or Alissa;

Le monstre

since, after Lafcadio, he must arrive in turn at Edouard (I give these names their full value as dynamic intellectual centers). And furthermore, what a vegetal sense of time! In the *Journal* many times we see Gide suspecting an early death; but his daimon knew otherwise from the start, knew the tree would achieve its full flowering crown in due course. So there is no rush, no improvisation, no swipes like those that make the trajectory of a Byron or a Balzac so anguished. Gide writes at the age of twenty what he should write at that age and only at that age; his forties deliver just the fragrance of the fruit; his sixties are deep, stylized, luxurious; his death arrives like the last page of the book that contains them all; foreseen, necessary, almost comfortable.

Unconsciously, but with a sure coenesthesia, Gide arranges his life and distributes within it, at harmonious distances, the products of that culture—cultivation—that are his books. His thought, his judgement, his style (which unites them) and his life are ruled by a divine proportion. The golden rule, in Gide, consists in being born of itself, like the shape of the tree; his tormented search has the Pascalian virtue of already being an encounter, of going off in the direction of what he already intimately is, in order to *deserve to be* who he is.

Ambulatory writer. As Rivière studied in Rimbaud, every stroll in the air and the sun excites my senses—*par les sens on va à la page*. After walking for a while I begin *to correspond to myself*, the tree is finally a tree, and the face of a woman or a kid glows with a sense that the rapid application of the label "passerby" hid from me earlier.

I have lunch at a cheap restaurant on Paraguay: *"Buen Amigo"* like Julio De Caro's lovely tango. I watch the street from my table, a lady checking through her purse, so thoroughly, a foot on tiptoe to make her thigh into a shelf, kids coming home from school. I feel a momentary fulfillment, absorbing the scene the window displays. In a perfect balance, the scene and I sweetly don't take part.

Then, the dissatisfaction of thinking I'm wasting this irretrievable moment of my irretrievable life watching a dark and vulgar corner of the city erupts voicelessly in my head. Other eyes at this instant will be looking at the spires of Chartres, the willows of Upsallata, the blues of Lorenzo Monaco, the face of Rosamund Lehmann.

Argos, with his thousand eyes: desperate myth of mankind. Never proven suspicion that we are but one single being; that I too am seeing (like in *El Zahir*) all that I love, but separated from my sight by guilt, by my origins.

Argos, human desire to see everything at once, here, now.

Chorus for *The Frogs* 1950:

—Kodak kodak kodak coca coca coca cola cola cola kodak coca cola kodak coca kodak cola . . .

A dream for which there aren't even any, not just words, litter-alness, but values, graspable angles, position. What's left to say is a miserable residue: A vaguely "colonial" plaza

    the night

                as always, abstract notations of a totality

    heat

                unnamed, a pure present being

    silence

On the floor—tiles or stone—a sinuous line, like something left by a giant slug, making loops, arabesques.

    I follow the line

    but at the same time I'd already followed it, because *that was my writing*, something I'd written on the floor

    notion that it must be important, that it counted.

    Then, something like a decision to read what was written (pre-viously

    —but there was no previously, everything was at once—

    I'd only looked, I suppose, without reading)

    And when I was going to read

I saw on the floor that my writing was no longer anything but a damp ribbon formed by condensation, little drops of water, nothing intelligible.

I didn't get upset; it was something else, a feeling that doesn't exist on this side.

Morning reflection: I've always liked to write and draw on misted up windows. Such flowing matter, as the drawing progresses the outside light takes pleasure in the line and shines right through.

After a while, the drawing drips, it is reduced to a formless pile of tears. The faces decay, fall apart.

Corollary: what happened to the portrait of Dorian was that Basil had painted it with his finger on a misty window, and he forgot to warn the model,

perhaps thinking it obvious because

Dorian was painted like that too, poor guy.

With the Musician, at Mimí's house. Conventional dinner, conversation that is always a *substitution*. The unbearable anguish of every silence longer than a second, threatening to lengthen. It's that if it lasts, we'd *look at each other*. (The so familiar faces that one day, in the purest instant, we suddenly see as they are, and how they instantly withdraw into their expression—the one we put on.)

Later the Musician plays with the piano, and Mimí sings Schumann, as well as Lieder by Mahler, and *Le promenoir des deux amants*; a tall lamp illuminates them. From the semi-darkness, in a half dream that only includes their golden and immaculate image, I listen to them. Now they are truly themselves, now when they're not themselves but the music. Tense, but with that release of tension that takes shape with luxury and devotion, they enter into the game as if it were always the first time. They discover, differ, advance, and the music seems to be using them to look at itself; I suspect it's alighted in Mimí's voice; happy to be happiness; and the pianist attacks and the piano responds, but the order emerging from his hands is—how to say it—parallel to the execution, analogous through difference; the pianist plays and the music is.

The lamp cloaks them, protects their joy. They play, *ils jouent*. I see Mimí's right hand helping to ascertain the melody on the piano (they're reading something for the first time). The hand proceeds with a subtle trial and error, an anticipation of the adjacent topography. I look at her little finger, slightly raised while the other fingers knit notes together; then it falls, precisely, on a D. The hand goes higher, other geometries emerge, and the little finger remains sort of aloof, until suddenly suspended again in its earlier position, repeats the note, withdraws . . .

And all this happens without Mimí (her attention on her voice, in her eyes) knowing. Only I see these rhythms weave themselves in space. Only I witness the ordering of her body in a way that is not her own, yet so much hers. Yes, the artist is the one who *concedes*; and the quality of the concession gives the measure of their art. So many ways to place a finger on a keyboard, and just one where the musical sign and the attentive abandon of the interpreter coincide to create the ground that is no longer them, that uses them: *Lieder*, poem, painting.

(I'm not confusing creator and interpreter; I'm talking about that occasional and marvelous instance where there is no longer any difference.)

The pleasure of travel does not stem so much from the admission into the unknown as from the rejection of habitual circumstances, which exceeds geography and already forms a part of us, like the air trapped in the treetop has its smell and its color and is the impalpable cast of its shape.

Sometimes they speak of "witnesses," of the daily watch a journey suppresses. It's a way of alluding to what Sartre called *"le regard"*; but I think there's something even worse. The environment of my life causes me sudden horror because it is my irreparable petrifaction, the proof that I am *this* and not A or B. To travel is to invent a spatial future. Instead, if I stay, I destroy even the temporal future to replace it with a matchbox future, a future of weekends, new detective stories, Thursdays with Olga and Sundays at the cinema. I know how many shirts I have in the closet. That wall of my office is a vertebra. Soup, then soup. Then this blue armchair.

(A tango:

Always the same, busy signal . . .
—Waiter, bring me a coffee
and tell me how much!)

The journey is no solution. Don't be so stupid as to believe that. Its—enormous—worth lies in reformulating the problems. Anyone who goes off and comes back, and has kept their eyes open, will know better the size of their cage, the angles and the steps that prepare escape.

Why do we still read Mansilla, Payró and Eduardo Wilde? For the same reason that will defend *Adán Buenosayres* from oblivion: humor. (A virtue that, in the case of *Adán*, staunches so much sloppiness.) Argentine books are as boring as a game of fifteen-sweep. Brahms should have been born in Buenos Aires. Provincial literature is infinitely tedious, because the provincial saves his humor (and what a lot he's got, in the café, the club, in politics) for his own personal life, so his writing is *serious*, dead.

Theory of the epigraph.
  The epigraph almost always appears during or after the writing of the book or poem. Seldom does it bring about the writing. But it always influences, it marks the book from outside with a touch

of a sword on the shoulder. All my life I shall regret having been unworthy to write a book for this phrase from *Le Grand Ecart:* "*Il était de la race des diamants, qui coupe la race des vitres.*"

Navigating by imagination and humor one could put together a splendid anthology of available epigraphs, points of departure for some other, some time, some place. Today I found this one, in *L'invitée* by Simone de Beauvoir:

Le reste de temps, il était volontiers solitaire: il allait au cinéma, il lisait, il se baladait dans Paris en caressant de petits rêves modestes et têtus.

And this other one: "*Ce n'était pas gai d'être jeune en ces temps-ci.*"

To open a book untouched for years and find notes I wrote in the margin in green pencil (in mamá's house) or black ink (student days). Realizing I thought something and wrote it, and now faced by the same text, I don't think that or I think something else entirely. Availability of intelligence. A given thing, which in itself does not change, causes contrary, secondary or merely analogous effects. Was it really me who wrote that? What special connection tied me to the book that day? The color of my mother's living room? My *robe de chambre?* How do they weigh on this reflection I no longer share, which I barely accept as possible—nothing to do with me?

I had a ceramic glass in my hand, a dark shiny green that in my memory has become more of a fragrance than a color. The fingers' pure delight at touching an exquisite object, exact encounter of reality with desire. All beauty gives me double recognition. The shape or support might surprise me; but I recognize something beautiful as something already mine. A shapeless desire just discovered it and separated it: because its shape was that one, and then I know it.

Endopathy—Certainly one projects; also in projecting oneself, one *returns*.

Good day, Plato, good day.

The halitosis of the soul that certain phrases reveal, not for any inherent reason, simply due to the intonation, the way of slipping them in, the gesture that accompanies them.

The opposite of reality is reality.

If we don't believe it through reason (which searches for and reaches its truth, not always ours), our skin leads us to believe it, to accept its confusing and continuous contention. *I feel it in my bones:* then one doubts no more. What my solar plexus tells me

but the thing is that its irrefutable force comes from the fact that it doesn't *tell* me: it gives me the thing itself, it enters into that order that is me. I can deny what I think; if I deny an anxiety or a striking revelation that immerses me in marvel or fright, I lapse into bad faith.

All this because a little while ago, coming down the courthouse steps into Plaza Lavalle, I suddenly felt that I had already died. I don't believe in immortality, and I really regret it (a bit like I regret that Claudel nauseates me, or that suits are expensive); but out of the blue I'm hit by the certainty that, in some shape, in some state, I have already passed through death.

An analogous state could be the remote basis for the belief in immortality. Today it's not so easy to accept and ride out the consequences; I believe in the state, in the authenticity of my experience (which here includes both senses of the word); but I cannot faithfully go on to infer a conviction. I only know that I have died before; nothing more. What guarantee do I have for the future? Maybe one revives twice, or twenty-eight times. Perhaps I'm on my last life. What right do I have to postulate immortality when the only thing I know is that I'm coming from one death?

Long talk with Juan about the Argentine idiom. He thinks it's better to speak of the *language*, inasmuch as it avoids all supposition of schism, which would be idiotic. "But you know very well that idiocies are always dangerously plausible," he tells me, "and that's why it's advisable to proceed from a very strict terminology." Then, with many examples that kept occurring to him all the while, most of which came from his own poems, he explained his linguistic trajectory, which otherwise corresponds to mine. It seems to both of us that only visual prejudices keep us on the side of *"gallina"* and *"verano,"* when we actually pronounce chicken as *gazhina* and summer as b*erano*, but that the visual dictatorship will not give way in our lifetime what the ear had given up since—I suppose—the times of Viceroy Vértiz.

—In reality it doesn't matter much—says Juan—since we grant ourselves full expressive liberty orally, even though our spelling still wears tails.—And he immediately began cursing porteño novelists who insist on using *tú*.

—They're like rotten old classical ballet—he says.—Still wearing the tutu.

—Well, we mix up vos and tú when we talk—I tell him.

—Of course we do, and that's fine. Sometimes I say *"qué querés"* and sometimes it comes out *"qué quieres."* That takes shape within the rhythms of the language, and if it happens to convey a last-minute indecision, a border, I don't see why we have to deny it when writing. What matters is not having a hieratic and a demotic and falling into the monstrosity of narrating the demotic with the hieratic. It's almost puerile having to keep repeating the basics—and he gets visibly angry.—But the sordid manoeuvring we do here with language gives the measure of what happens underneath. Like everything that happens to us, this has ethical roots, old man.

I point out to him that the problem has many facets, and one of them is the leukaemia that is making the language we speak increasingly anaemic. There's a tendency to laugh at the attempts at blood transfusion reflected by, for example, a book like *La guerra gaucha*. But notice—I tell Juan—that Don Leopoldo seems to have realized what's going on, and tried a sort of great funfair of words, in the style of TWO HUNDRED LOCUTIONS TWO HUNDRED, to see if he could shove up our noses, with big trombone slides and flares, tons of displaced words.

—It's a question of fear—says Juan.—You know the horror we feel at the slightest whiff of pedantry. One time I wrote in a sonnet, speaking of the sun: *King, albescent plumed light, incandescent plectrum!*—you should have seen the things I had to listen to. Here we accept "light of white feathers," but nuts to the other.

—You'll admit your verbiage is rather Gongo-rine.

—Of course I admit it. But in a sonnet, man . . . (You can tell he still likes it.)

—You're right about the fear—I tell him.—We've invented a substitution of language, a kind of system of references not so much to the mentioned objects but to the primitive signs. You often have to lift the first layer of words to attend to the second; in this dangerous operation what usually happens is that the objective correlate gets diluted or loses importance. We read essays about an essay on something; it's terrible how far away the something gets left . . .

—Fear forms an alliance with laziness—says Juan.—It's already a *cliché* to point out we're writing on loan. We extract from the sciences all sorts of rigorous verbal formulas, which we use in the hope of trapping the increasingly evasive facts that interest us. Laziness invents monsters: images. Since we don't know or we spurn or fear to use the Spanish word that mentions an object, we surround it with an image.

—So, you'd be for a richer language?

—Look, there are no rich or poor languages—says Juan—but there are greater or lesser expressive needs. *La guerra gaucha* is a sad, roughly painted balloon, because it responds formally to an *ex nihilo* invention; you must have noticed how hymns to gods are always very ornamental. I think we shouldn't be afraid to use all the albescent plumage that occurs to us, as long as it comes to the aid of the so-called expressive need, don't you?

—But we've forgotten so many words. Dictionaries are columbariums, catacombs.

—It's not such a bad idea to visit dictionaries—says Juan, giving me a sidelong glance.—It may not seem like it, but there are loads of things that live virtually, waiting for their sign. One fine day you find that the word you've glanced at distractedly in an enormous alphabetical list, turns up at the perfect moment and gets you out of a jam.

—You're too nominalistic—I tell him.—You see ideas and words like nuts and bolts.

—Here come the mechanics. But no, *che*, on the contrary, I think we get to the idea through the word, and that in general our sad language, so badly learned and worse in practice, guides our thought.

—Well, I don't—I answer him.—I always write with the idea a little ahead of the word. I have the same problem as that little kid Roger Fry asked about his drawings. The kid said: *First I think and then I draw a line around my think.*

—The line was already there—says Juan, petulantly.—You and that kid do nothing more than trace it with the pencil.

Nocturnal supplement to part of this conversation:

"*Mais nous voici en train de rendre compte d'une étude de Maurice Blanchot sur un texte de Heidegger, qui lui-même rend compte d'un poème de Hölderlin . . .*" (Jean-Jacques Salomon, reviewing a book by Blanchot in *Le temps modernes*.)

This literature of mirrors stems from a fascination with De Quincey and Mallarmé. No one here has done better than Borges at measuring this distancing the spirit sets up to surmise its sophistry on a plane where the elements are closer to him than to crude reality. The invention of a mental object is always deceptive: a Quangle Wangle does not replace a tiger. That's why one prefers to *receive* that tiger who's passed through two or three books, who is Shere Khan, who in a sonnet from the *Neue Gedichte* lodges and loses in his grim heart the image of the one who watches him, and comes to us as pure *tigerness*.

(As a boy I marvelled at the passage from *Les mariés de la Tour Eiffel* where a tiny tiger the size of a sugar cube goes for a walk around a wedding cake. Someone explained: "It's a mirage; the tiger exists and he's taking a walk, *grandeur nature*, on the other side of the ocean.")

I could never manage to write the story that would show this overlapping of literature with objectivity, and at the same time the voluntary breaking off, that *deep down hates realism*. The idea is a man seated on a green sofa beside a big window overlooking a park, reading a novel in which a woman meets her lover furtively, agrees on the need to kill her husband so they can be free, and climbs the stairs that will take her to the room where the husband, sitting on a green sofa, beside a window, reads a novel . . .

(S.W. has a version of this story, but I should burn it.)

On degrees of love. There are things one remembers loving, but cannot now update, cannot tolerate face to face. I'm moved by the memory of *Old Black Joe*, but I only have to whistle it to deplore its incurable stupidity. That's why I'll never reread my Jules Verne; I sometimes just dare to peek at one or two of Roux's prints, the boys from *Adrift in the Pacific* or Isaac Hakkabut's tartan in *Hector Servadac*.

To love in memory—There's not exactly a memory, but rather emotions and feelings remain attached in our memory to the desired subject in question. The special tonality of this love: what makes it so penetrating is that it serves as a living and current feeling applied to a similar subject. To *feel* today what was then—(Terrible and marvelous imbalance between the child's capacity for love and the minute value of what he loves. A cat, a little figure, a caress, the end of a story, a glass ball . . . The almost ineffable realization that we pass indifferently by the shop window shiny with multicolored spheres, while in our memory sleeps the intense love for a sphere that no longer exists.)

> *Thank heaven I never was sent to a school*
> *To be flogged into following the style of a fool.*
> William Blake

A sentence to slip, as a surprise, delight or scandal (depending on the reader) into any note on influences: "The most successful of Marc Allegret's works is a novel called *The Counterfeiters.*"

Every once in a while to read a book of pure metaphysics. Heimsoeth, Scheler, Heidegger. Like taking a sulphur springs cure. Cleanses, fixes and gives . . . No, it doesn't give; it takes away, which is what's needed.

Influence of cinema on dreams. I noticed a cinematic framing in a nightmare a couple of hours ago; what's more, I was aware while I was dreaming it. I don't remember much; the dream is a nightmare when a minimum number of situations become charged with such an enormous symbolism that each mutation is a new emotional shock that can't be sustained for very long. The later recounting is always deceptive (note that a nightmare can be preceded by a long dream, that we'll remember in detail; but even though, Wagnerianly, the themes of the horror are already hanging around, only at the end do they leap out in full orchestra. The pure nightmare cannot last long, it would kill us.)

I remember a room from this one—that is: I know it was one —and a stretcher or a morgue table where there was a corpse. Some fat, tall person had been occupied there (autopsy?) and when

I looked—here's the cinematic part, because I was looking down from above, like the camera that films moving horizontally while shooting from top to bottom—I couldn't see anything because they were covering the corpse with black velvet at the same rate that my gaze moved down from the head to the toes. With perfect pace, almost as if my eyes were emitting the velvet an instant before the gaze itself.

Then it seems I went to move further away, and at that moment I felt myself hurled into the air (without anyone grabbing me, but sure that it was the same fat individual) and I felt—I think the sensation was at once visual and physical—that my path through the air would end up on the marble table, I felt like a carpet unrolling, a solid log that suddenly turns into a two-dimensional sheet. Confusing impression of: "but then of course, I'm that (corpse)" and the horror. I woke up in the very act of being left lying on the slab.

All this could be filmed, the first part as I described it, the second with a rapid sequence of looks, shadows and movement. (Send a letter to Lumitón.)

If, as Eliot says, an emotion can only be transmitted by way of a system of meanings and correlatives recreated in the reader, I'd like to write a novel that communicates rage. No, an objectified rage, a rage in action. Here the reasons for rage are of such a low grade that they defeat their adversary by inanity. The viscous enrages more than the thorny; it generates a rage of low tones, a strained rage that feeds on official speeches and palace gossip, that lets off steam with little cups of coffee, bitter recounting, comparisons with times gone by (which were better).

That's why the novel I'm imagining should translate this rage surreptitiously, without anything in its appearance suggesting it. That the reader might know (when my sad, vain, subequatorial rage emerges by analogy from the situations) that this is the theme and the *raison d'être* of the story. And that the novelist, as Sartre believed, having chosen a secondary mode of action, is making signals in his book to incite the reader's rage to be, if possible, more effective than his own.

Write the novel of nothing. Let everything play out in such a way that the reader senses that the horrible theme of the work is that of not having one.

Show the most secret (although today it appears in public) of human suspicions: that of their intrinsic, inherent futility.

Insinuate that the religion of the work (in its highest values: art, poetry) is also *sport*. Thump hypocrisies.

Physical impossibility of listening to Chopin. Disgust, revulsion.

Don't fall into the error of attributing to the musician the reasons for this disgust that only today — and only for me — hold water.

But don't invent a connection where there isn't one either, and hypocritically sustain the alibi of art's timelessness. Art is indeed timeless, but I'm not. If Perotin or Guillaume Machault fit into my time and there's no room for Schubert, it's because my transience affirms itself as the center of the wheel, and throws out the radii of the analogy, looking for its own outside of time, but

watch

from within time: this one.

My time being me, or I my time, constitutes another problem. The solution in the next incarnation.

(Corollary for Monday's *Wagneriana:* If there is a gentleman beside me whose time includes Chopin, that doesn't mean that his time has anything to do with mine. Coexisting is not coinciding.)

Julien Benda, or Epictetus in the whorehouse.

As if in dreams one sometimes might achieve the necessary purity to trap essences, waking from certain dreamed fables leaves the astonished anxiety of returning from the sea, from a peak, from the origins. Paula dreamed of the return of the first day—which will occur on the last, on what they call the Day of Judgement. First she saw a character from a story of mine, on the steps of the faculty of Philosophy and Letters, but there was no longer any faculty or any steps, just the plain with the river in the background; for the Final Judgement everything was back to being what it really was, and the truth of men had given way before the smoothness of the pampas, water and earth meeting again with no limit other than their own. The earth was left, free of its historical attire, of products.

In the other dream, Paula heard a dead friend who spoke to her by telephone. She was happy, telling her so many cheerful things. Disturbed, Paula asked her brother later: "How is it possible? You know how anguished she was before she died; and now, talking to me with such joy . . ."

"But now it's the Final Judgement," he answered, "and she's gone back to what she truly was."

Inhabited by words, by events, by whole chapters, this consciousness is a corridor and an eye at the far end watching bugs and sounds go by, a monotonous parade of tango lyrics, detached lines and little bits of faces and rough drafts.

There are lines that chase me from all sides, they go away for a while and return with more enthusiasm. They're presences I have to carry around in my hand, in the leather headband of my hat, in the smallest section of my wallet, mixed up with stamps and photo-booth pictures; like Michaux's little lock-eating animal; you have to take them by the hand and let them eat something every once in a while, even if it's the words they're made of.

Since last night I've got this line by Patrick Waldberg in my head:

Par le coeur cloué sur une ruine

and nothing more, I have to fill in the rest, or just hear it coming and going. It's a good bug, like a cricket or a ladybug; a lovable insect.

In a diary of life you don't relate the deaths.

A good epigraph for the novel I'd like to write:

"One finds among the ruins themselves and in the active demolitions a great number of human bones, many of the skulls still with hair attached, pieces of the vessels that they would have used, and among these things a large net, made of twine, torn away in places, which can be recognized as having been used for fishing, these things being all that remains after the many pieces of some interest, and others of value that have been removed by those occupied in the razing of the buildings, the charm of which has not ceased, exerting itself from time to time on some of those who commit themselves to continuing the demolition."

Antonio de Ulloa, *Noticias Americanas*,

Entertainment XX

Stoicism on paper. I wish the gesture of death wouldn't burst in from outside, that it wouldn't amplify itself disproportionately; that between putting a fork or a pistol to my mouth there wouldn't be so much qualitative difference. If killing yourself is a window, not to go out knocking at the door. If living were *not a bang but a whimper*, prepare the cessation of activities with the same simplicity as turning off the bedside lamp to admit one more night. The period is tiny, and almost invisible on the written page; you notice it later by contrast, when the white begins beyond it.

Every Stoa is a technique, a habituation. Going along with no pre-conceived intention, but sure

(without thinking about it, like the pianist is sure of what will come twenty bars ahead)

that at any moment, for no reason in fact, the gesture will simply happen, halfway through a cigarette, after the last conversation, or a farewell, or a concert.

Not a battle—already fought so long ago—just an account balance, that no one is demanding urgently, that we could postpone. Or a battle (so as not to feel already so resigned) but like the opal Fargue evokes, where *le jour et la nuit luttent avec douceur.*

For the anthology of epigraphs:

C'est une de ces âmes tendres qui ne connaisant pas la manière de tuer le chagrin, se laissent toujours tuer par lui.

Balzac, *Gobseck*

La grande fatigue de l'existence, n'est peut-être en somme que cet énorme mal qu'on se donne pour demeurer vingt ans, quarante ans, davantage, raissonnable, pour ne pas être simplement, profondement soi-même, c'est-à-dire immonde, atroce, absurde.

Celine, *Voyage au bout de la nuit*

I met someone called Salaver, who the chronicler calls the Chinese guy. Absurd and tiresome demonstration of his struggle against fate. In short it consists in postulating a given future order, fixing it as the sole choice. Against this Salaver then applies his special magic.

Hollow conversation, weak and verging-on-incoherent individual. But I can't avoid the sensation that his presence last night was less fortuitous than it appeared. In everything he said, without his knowledge, there was news, a piece of advice, something that escapes me —

Observe
  (I write to not think about anything other than what I'm proposing)
                                                                    heat
that the creator is responsible for the future. Contrary to the Chinese guy, who would like to freeze unfolding time to frustrate it with a free and personal plan, the painter or the musician adds a further element, active and living, to the virtual pulse of the future. When painting, from among all the possibilities choosing one that enters through that instant in the future. Where you see it best is in works from an unknown or underestimated time (the gothic, for example) that suddenly explode in all their current power. When I look at an image from Chartres, I am seeing the future of that statue; it is so wrong to talk of ancient art. And the little figure of Gudea with the plan in his hands isn't five thousand years of age; it's five thousand years ahead of its age.

No, it's not enough to cower behind the well-organized, what gets you out of a jam, your machine to fabricate ideas. Atrocious dissociation, thinks

and I   the heat   Gudea, little figure,   interesting deductions.
And the fog, Andrés?

The fog surrounds the house. It's noon, I've just spoken to Clara who wanted me to go to a concert. When I told her no I was watching the fog piled up in the window; it's so hot that you can't keep the house closed up, but opening a window is to feel enveloped in that dirty dust of lukewarm wool.

Tricks: continue, by substitution, a description that replaces the other thing. Not even here can I—Bah, the writing brings with it its destiny of being read; I even regret having given Juan my notebook last night, I miss this loose page, this paper where the pen advances with slight cracklings,

imitation fabric,

and when he gives it back I'll surely paste the page back in, or I'll copy it out scholastically,

if there's time, which

The need to get out on the street. Free, absolutely free outside myself. I told her I didn't want to go with them, although in the evening,

and this other thing I said because, now I see so clearly, I was disguising my need to see her again under the pretext of self-denial, of going to accompany her to the exam.

The innermost fabrics of treachery. The virtues, the obverse that passes for reverse. So, I'll go,

head out onto the street, like a need to reach the center of the fog, to be the fog looking at itself, smelling itself, this that destroys itself

(poor old chronicler, full of hopes for explanation—To have time to talk to the chronicler; but yet another pretense).

To go out, with total availability in your pocket. Stella (who doesn't exist) sings in the kitchen, lunch, you're sweating, that tie looks really nice on you, order, order.

What's this, Andrés? You, always so careful, so dressy, so Aristotelian. The fog, Andrés, the fog?

I should accept her voice, what she was trying to tell me behind her words. I never did justice to Clara's delicate modesty, her fear of weighing too heavily on anyone's arm. I imposed my reluctance on her, my not wanting to go, but that was something else,

not even that stupidity about Abelito,

claiming a closeness to me that by last night—

The fog, Andrés? Look how it distorts that tree, like Stella's voice coming from the kitchen sounding padded and murky. If I'm imagining things, if just behind, in shadow, is Clara   pure picture of her name,

the dexterous matador who doesn't err when he strikes, because he neither hates nor belittles

because simply the sword

as simply as this clumsy longing sponge   me

Bah, a shower and out the door. The paper's run out and although

Book Design by David Bullen Design
Printed by The Stinehour Press, Lunenburg, Vermont